Klaus Landahl

Crash 85

AF145418

The Story

A fictional tale about a man's attempts to be a leaf in order to stay alive. Who is the man named Cissie Trump? And what about the young woman with the long blonde hair coming out of the past? Can the transformation of a man into a leaf really help solve his problems?

Crash 85 is a work of fiction. Names, characters, places, and incidents are the products of the author's imagination or are used fictitiously. Any resemblance to actual events, locales, or persons, living or dead, is entirely coincidental.

The Author

Klaus Landahl is a German writer. He has five children and lives in the north of Germany. This novel is his first attempt at a spiritual book in the English language.

In his own words: "There was no need for me to be perfect. I chose to write this book in English because writing in another language allows my mind to think in a different way. By doing so, I free myself from the confines of my own culture and gain insight into other cultures and perhaps even in its memories, too. My daughter Annika Lena was so kind as to help me with the dictionary."

The illustrations in this book are by the author.

Klaus Landahl

CRASH 85

A Man's Attempts to be a Leaf in Order to Stay Alive

TWENTYSIX

Bibliographical Information of the Deutsche Nationalbibliothek:

This publication is listed in the Deutsche Nationalbibliografie of the Deutsche Nationalbibliothek; detailed bibliographical information can be accessed under http: // dnb.d-nb.de.

TWENTYSIX – der Self-Publishing Verlag
A cooperation between Verlagsgruppe Random House and Books on Demand, Norderstedt, Germany

© 2020 Landahl, Klaus

Cover art: SK-Studio/Shutterstock.com
Proofreading: www.lektorat-westhoff.de
Printing and Production:
BoD – Books on Demand, Norderstedt, Germany

ISBN: 978-3-7407-6940-6

First,
a Personal Remark
by the Protagonist Mr. Nor Lung
Alias Male Female

Our world is like a door
swimming in the sea
below the sky
amidst the universe and
my fate is to be
one of a billion nails in this door
or a leaf
in the wide ocean of God's love.

But I wonder
whether to be a nail or a leaf
could be more
than a mirage.

Second,
a Remark by the Author

'Crash 85' should be able
to withstand the test of time,
passing from one community to another
I was waiting for months but
I didn't reach the right feeling for it
because of my own situation
amidst a pandemic world.

It was the early morning
between the end of sleeping and the real awake,
when there came another story to my mind,
the story of
Mr. Nor Lung alias Male Female,
of Mr. Beggar alias Cissie Trump and
of a very young woman
coming out of the past.

The only thing I could do was become aware of it
and keep it in mind until breakfast.

Index

Part One

Alone

CHAPTER 1

Two men were walking along a hallway which had some windows on the left and black doors on the right. One of the men stopped.

"Now, Mr. Nor Lung," he said. "Here we are. This is the door of your room. Until I give you a sign, you must stay in it."

Room number 39, right?

"No, the next door, please. Number 40. By the way, you have got a new name for the duration of your stay in our residence. You'll find it inside the room, nailed on the door."

Mr. Nor Lung seemed to be a little surprised and hesitant.

A new name? What for? And why nailed on a door? That's a bit strange, isn't it?

"Just an order, sir. Good luck and have a pleasant stay."

No, no! Just a moment, please. Don't leave! I'm not sure about being in such a mysterious room and, moreover, getting a new name. My name is Nor Lung. You said it yourself just a few minutes ago.

The other man smiled and answered in a gentle voice,

"You wanted to stay here for a few days in order to find your way back to life, sir, didn't you? Remember, you are searching for some support to stay alive."

The two men stared into each other's eyes. Finally, Mr. Nor Lung turned to the door, sobbing.

Yes, okay, you are right, he replied. *Nevertheless, it's an unusual ambiance, the bright floor with the black doors. The door to my room doesn't even have a number. I wonder whether this room could help me. How can I be sure that this is all true?*

"It's just my order to open this room for you, sir. So, please hand over your watch and enter the room."

Stop! Sorry, only one more question. Why is the number 40 not outside my door?

"Don't worry. You won't leave your room anyway. Well, it's really time for us to go our separate ways now, isn't it, sir?"

The man named Nor Lung entered the room and the door was locked immediately. He stood in grey darkness, with only a candle on the floor for light.

Then he saw his new name pinned to the inside of the door: Male Female. Above it there was the missing number: 40.

CHAPTER 2

Now he was alone in a great silence. Male opened the curtains, looking for a window, but there was only a wall. He looked around. This room didn't have any windows.

He picked up the candle to better inspect the room. It was small and had no bed, no water, no table, no refrigerator, not even a phone. Only one chair stood in the middle of the room. Mr. Nor Lung tried to open the door, but it was still locked.

The candle started flickering. Then the room disappeared into absolute darkness.

Male knocked at the door to no response. Some minutes later he knocked once more, shouting,

Hello! The candle's out! And what about a window? I'm standing in the dark! I can't see any electric lights, not even an electric chair, ha!

He knocked more vehemently, and stomped his foot on the door.

Suddenly an unknown voice reached his ears from behind the wall. It sounded like an Australian didgeridoo,

"Shut up, stupid man, don't be silly, just look around. Don't you see the curtains?"

Male stopped pounding on the door and turned his body around to the curtains again. Now there was a window behind it.

That was alarming! Where did the window come from?

Male's room was in the second story. He opened the window carefully and looked down into a bright and sunny garden. Old trees were planted amid a lovely fountain. A young woman with long blonde hair stood nearby.

He was surprised when the woman looked up to him, shouting,

"Hi, Male, long time no see."

Male didn't remember ever meeting this young woman. But the moment she spoke to him and said his new name he began to feel a little bit happy, free even.

The young woman sensed the shift in his mood and laughed, calling,

"Be careful, my love, there is not only no light in your room, but also no loo either!"

Male panicked at once. He needed a loo. Absolutely! How could he redeem the promise of his life without a loo?

During his panic, the woman continued laughing. Suddenly, the window disappeared just in front of his nose and the laughing was interrupted. It was a bitter moment of deja vu for him and he stood there in the dark, upset, touching the terrible wall.

Where was the unknown woman now, who called him 'my love'?

As Male fumbled for the door, his neighbour's voice appeared again,

"Hey, stupid man, is the window gone again? Not so good, is it? That's for you, living in my former room. Number 39 where I have to live now, doesn't have any windows. Someone will explain."

I didn't know that. So sorry. What's your name in this residence?

"They tried to wash me away. They call me Cissie Trump."

Oh!

"They are a gang. They said I'm an uncontrollable child in a man's body. They are trying to change my mind. Fools."

Who are they?

"They want to change me from a nasty child into a man, ha."

Instead of an answer, Male Female shouted,

I have no bed in my room! I can't sleep on the ground. Do you have a bed?

But there came no answer from room 39.

Male Female stood a few minutes irresolutely in the dark. Then he laid down in a corner of his room, trying to fall asleep and worrying about how to stay alive in such a poor company.

CHAPTER 3

Male Female was woken up early in the morning by bright sunshine from an open window, and the wonderful smell of coffee and scrambled eggs, all placed on the chair.

He sat up. This couldn't be true! It was incredible! When he got up and ran to the window, he discovered a hole in the corner next to his sleeping place. It was the loo.

He squatted down in front of the chair and started his breakfast.

When he'd finished the meal, the window disappeared as well. Male was in darkness again. He sat down on the floor and wanted to be a leaf, outside this room and far away from all kinds of people.

That was the reason he had to stay in this residence.

Male Female was not able to believe in his ability to continue his life as a man, so his mind opened to the possibilities of other kinds of life.

In fact, time hung heavy on his hands. He feared that in this residence there would also be no end of trouble for him.

In that minute, like a run of bad luck, there was once more the awful didgeridoo voice from behind the wall.

"Hey number next to me! Are you awake? How's the weather behind your window? I no longer have the privilege to see the sky. They mean – ha – ha – that no human rights exist to see the sky nor be rich or live in endless prosperity or to be an owner of people. Bullshit I say! Bullshit! Someone will explain!"

Male Female didn't answer. This weird didgeridoo man obviously had far more problems than he had.

"Hey", his neigbour continued, "guy in my former room, don't decide to stop listening to me! The guys here tried to explain to me that the economy needs people only in order to eat them, first as labour material and then as customer material. These guys will never be able to think great! They are losers. Fools. They will expiate!"

What do they mean? The economy gives us prosperity! We are not victims!

"Every day when you act as a consumer, you protect the rich, you forget the poor and you dismantle democracy. All day long you act as a part of the economy, but are only seldom a part of democracy. You know it, but you let it run. That's what they say."

Are you sure they are wrong?

"Well, yes I am. The economy is very powerful, ha."

CHAPTER 4

Male's time passed away, day and night and another day and night, slowly, silently. There was not even any noise from the didgeridoo's room. Darkness all day, a depressing darkness and no chance to obtain any food.

One morning Male Female woke up to a vision of daylight surrounding him.

At first he kept his eyes closed, full of surprise and fear, but when he felt fresh air touch his face, he quickly sat up.

On the chair awaited him a new breakfast, but his sole impulse was only to see the sunny garden with the fountain and, perhaps, maybe, the young woman.

So he stood at the window, surrounded by daylight and fresh air, when he saw her. She was looking up at him, waving.

"Male, my love, come down and speak to me", she said.

Male stared at her and answered,

Sorry, young girl. The door is locked so I can't leave my room. And I'm very hungry.

She laughed.

"Have a cup of tea and then come down."

It's impossible!

"Try it, my love, don't let your great-grandmother wait!"

Male didn't understand why she would make such a joke at this moment, but he obeyed her. He went to the door, touched the handle and his prison actually opened. At once, Male hastened through the hallway, jumping down the stairs until he came to a stop.

There was the woman. They stood opposite each other, face to face. The young woman didn't laugh any longer, but she stood and stared at him.

She seemed to be much younger than Male had expected, no older than 15. She was really very pretty, but her way of dress was rather old fashioned, even in the eyes of a layman of women's fashion like Male.

He stood there like a fool. She was so young, so alive and all the future was in her possession. Male lost his courage. He meekly said,

I think we've never met before. Sorry for calling you 'girl'.

"A long time ago, I was young in reality. I had a little girl myself. Time had passed. You are her great-grandchild, so I saw you crying for help."

What do you mean, you had a little girl? You yourself are so young. It's impossible for you to be a grandmother.

"I never struggled for love. I have seen in men's eyes neither danger nor safety."

Suddenly, Male saw a speeding bicyclist coming closer and closer at high speed.

Watch out! he hastily called out to the woman. *Watch out for the biker behind you! Move aside, quickly!*

To the biker he exclaimed,

Hey! This isn't a motorway!

The young woman didn't move and the biker passed through her body. Male yelled in shock.

"Did you speak to me?" asked the biker, slowly circling around to face him.

I had a vision that you will crash with the young woman beside me.

"Don't share your stupid vision with other people. I have my own."

The woman remained unaffected by their exchange. She pointed at the fountain.

"Let us go and sit down there in order to talk about your problems, my love. You are a little nervous, aren't you?"

CHAPTER 5

The fountain stopped sprinkling the moment they sat down at its edge.

You are like a fountain, said Male, *You seem strange and yet also familiar. Who are you? Who sent you to me?*

"I am one of your ancestors, your very own great-grandmother. We come from a long line of forefathers. They watched over their descendants just as I watch over you. I heard your cry for help and have come to answer it."

Oh.

"Firstly, try to be as silent as the leaf you want to be."

A leaf? How do you know that? To become a leaf is a very silly idea.

"Not really. When you are dead, no kind of life is silly."

Why do you say that?

"Billions of leaves are present for just a little while, just like people. It's indisputable that every single leaf is necessary and important for life on earth."

There was a long pause. Finally Male said,

Perhaps it's not important for me any longer. One early morning I woke up and realized that I'm mortal. Mortal, you see. Dead, forgotten, nothing, a misty blast of wind, unable to save anyone, even my own life! I believe in God, but my heart has become full of sorrow! I feel terribly lonely, grandma.

The young woman looked at him with so much affection that Male began sobbing. He asked,

For how long has your life been passing away?

"My life had passed a long time before Jesus was born. I had never seen the men who came to us before. They conquered our camp."

Oh, no!

"It was a long time ago."

Oh, no!

"Well, it was only one of a billion other wars that continue even today. Now – shall I help you or do you need to talk some more?"

Sorry, grandma.

She laughed.

"Listen – don't call me grandma. My mother always called me 'Raingirl' because it was raining the day of my birth."

CHAPTER 6

"Son, you must know that my home is the origin of life. Women are the reason for all life on earth. Female means the 'first beginning'. Our life is a never ending brawl that continuously rages on between the men and women of the earth. But the sky and universe only need the earth. Evolution of the human essence will not happen within the next billion years. But, perhaps, there will be a chance for you."

In Male's heart was great confusion. He was very tired and full of sadness. There seemed to be so much wrong inside him. And he didn't understand what the young woman had meant.

She looked at him and said,

"Forget it, my love, it's only my sorrow. Sorrow for the male shade of death, greed and all kinds of simple stupidity. That's why you hope that you will have peace when you escape and change into a leaf."

Male was more and more fascinated by this young woman. She seemed to be a part of himself, coming out of the past with her wonderful name, 'Raingirl'. She was so friendly and tender. She gave him security and made him feel a little less negative.

He was impatient to hear more about the leaf. This could give him back his life, not only now but perhaps even a thousand years later again.

So he declared,

Show me how to change into a leaf.

"First, you should know that it will be a fallen leaf. You have to consider that it's still summertime. It's not the right moment for a leaf to fall down, you see?"

Go on!

"A leaf isn't alive from itself. When time is up, it has to descend from the tree. But it doesn't die."

Go on, please.

"Laying on the ground, it changes and becomes part of the earth as a home for hedgehogs during the winter and food for lots of little animals. It keeps the ground warm to save the new life that will come out of it in springtime, until it finally becomes the ground itself. The leaf is always in God's hand, just like you. It belongs to the earth and the sky with all the clouds."

That will really help me? It's hard to believe. But, go on, please.

"Believe in yourself, only then will you be free like a leaf. Free from greed, free for the sun and the moon, for all trees, grasses, flowers and love."

A leaf could fall in love, huh?

"That's the difference, my dear Male. You are a human being. We both can't love each other like a leaf still hanging on the tree or laying on the ground."

A silence rose around them.

Raingirl said hesitatingly,

"You will never be alone. Trust in the earth, trust in the leaves, trust in the day after the day. Trust not only the mighty mountains but also the smaller mounds."

When Male, tears in his eyes, bent to hug her, the fountain started sprinkling and its water took her away.

CHAPTER 7

"Mr. Female!"

The man who Male remembered from the day of his arrival was shouting for him.

"Come on, your time is up! You have already been with us for a full year."

Male stood up and slowly left the border of the fountain where the young woman had disappeared.

He was still confused as he followed the other man into the house. They walked along the hallway with all the windows on the left and a lot of numbered black doors on the right.

They stopped between room number 39 and room number 40, the former room of Male Female.

"Now, Mr. Nor Lung, here we are again. It's time for us to go our separate ways."

You won't call me Male Female any longer?

"Those are my instructions, sir."

By the way, congratulations! There is, at long last, the number 40 on the outside of the room.

"That's no longer your room, sorry, sir. Your room is number 39 until we've finished your discharge papers. Now, please, enter."

No! No! There is a didgeridoo man inside! And he told me that this room has no window!

"Aren't you a window yourself now, sir? But in reality, you have to leave us now and the only available room at the moment is number 39."

Mr. Nor Lung sighed. He touched the door handle, paused, and said,

I'm a little confused. I miss the young woman with the long blonde hair. I even couldn't say good bye to her. But now I will do my best. How long do I have to stay in room 39 before leaving your residence?

"You'll leave us at supper, sir."

41

Today's supper?

"Ha, yes, sir, sure, today's."

End of Part One

Part Two

Together

CHAPTER 8

One year later Mr. Nor Lung went again down the bright floor with the black doors on the right. He had decided to return to the residence. The man from the previous year was with him yet again.

The man stopped and said,

"Mr. Nor Lung, thanks again for joining us once more. Now, would you prefer room number 40 or 39 this time? I read in your file that you had very successful results from room 40 last year."

Hmm. Not really. Perhaps, yes, perhaps.

"Yes what, sir? 40 or 39? It's your choice. I think room 40 will be more enjoyable for you this time."

Anyone inside?

"Not yet. Somebody will arrive at noon. This late gentleman will get the one you choose not to take."

I'll take room 39 this time.

"Oh."

I'll enjoy number 39, I'm sure. By the way, no new name for me this year? Only my own?

"Yes sir. Just an order."

While the man opened the door he added,

"There is nothing inside, sir, neither a chair nor a bed. And no window and no radiator, too. It's a dark and cold room, but it has a loo in the right hand corner."

That should be enough.

Mr. Nor Lung entered. The door was immediately locked behind him. This year he wasn't afraid of the dark. He sat down on the floor, leaning his back against the cold wall and shutting his eyes.

The hours passed by very slowly. No noise came from room 40. Mr. Nor Lung tried to laugh. Then he used the loo.

He let all his feelings go away, his brain and soul becoming more and more empty.

Finally, he fell into a deep sleep.

CHAPTER 9

Mr. Nor Lung woke up with a fright. Someone was noisily knocking at the wall he was leaning against.

He heard a voice proclaim,

"Is there someone in 39? Answer! Who are you?"

That's the didgeridoo man! Mr. Nor Lung thought in surprise and replied,

I'm the guy from 40. I stayed in it last year.

"Ha! Better luck next time, buddy. Enjoy that dump of a room. I'm just looking out of my window to a wonderful and sunny, snow covered garden with old trees. There's even a frozen fountain and a snowman nearby. Wish I could share this with a poor guy like you."

Mr. Nor Lung only asked,

Do you also see a girl with long blonde hair near the fountain?

"Oh yes, with long legs and ..."

Shut up. You are talking about my great-grandmother.

"Really? Wow!"

I said shut up!

"I was just having fun. Sorry, buddy."

Mr. Nor Lung was surprised that the didgeridoo man was at the residence at the same time as himself, wall to wall. What reason could be behind such a phenomena?

He sat down against another wall and shut his eyes again. Last year when he had become a female within the body of a leaf, he had fallen right under a mouse's stomach. He was back within life. However, there was still an important hurdle he'd yet to conquer in this new life: he wasn't able to love.

Mr. Nor Lung woke up some time later, feeling nervous. The darkness of his room had begun to worry him. He could no longer see an advantage to being here, trying yet again to stay alive.

He was in a very bad mood.

He wanted to bask in daylight, he wanted to see his great-grandmother who had, just last year, appeared to him as a young woman named 'Raingirl'. He suddenly wasn't so sure it had been a prudent decision to pause his peaceful life as a leaf.

He said to himself,

A leaf must be free in order to feel female, but, perhaps, I am wrong. How can I speak with 'Raingirl'? I so wish to see her again.

These thoughts made it impossible for him to continue sleeping. The room was cold and the floor supremely uncomfortable to lie on. Then, his eyes abruptly caught a breeze of movement nearby.

Who's there? Come and let me see you!

Mr. Nor Lung started to blindly feel the area around him when, all of a sudden, his hand brushed against the branches of a coniferous tree.

A woman laughed.

"That's my present for you, my love, it's a Christmas tree with three candles, so you will have some light on this special evening."

Wow, you frightened me! I nearly had a heart attack. Please, let me see you, grandma, hmm, Raingirl. I'm so glad that you are back.

"Not yet. You have to wait until Christmas."

But I'm in need of your help now. I've changed into a leaf, yes, but it's impossible for me to forget that I'm a kind of human feeling leaf, you see? I still feel so much like a human being. I need some parts of my humanity further on. Do you understand what I mean? How can I make it possible to be both, to share and to connect?

"Did you already speak with the man in the next room?"

Number 40?

"Yes. Try to place your questions and your feelings in his hands."

That's impossible! He's a terrible didgeridoo man!

"Try it, my love, try it."

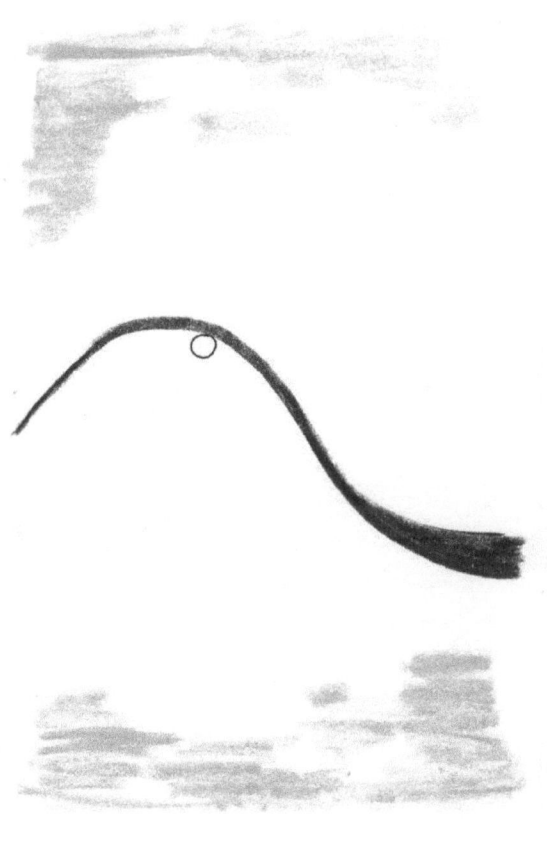

CHAPTER 10

Mr. Trump, can you hear me?

"Speak up, buddy. And my real name is Beggar. People used to call me 'Honest Beggar'. So stop calling me Trump."

Honest Beggar, I need your help.

"Hmm."

What did you say? Sorry, I didn't catch that.

"Why do you want to hear my voice? Is there anything worth hiding? Tell me, buddy."

No. Nothing at all.

"Why are you so impatient? The day is long and the night endless. Should I name your problems, guy?"

You? In reality you can't know my problems, Honest Beggar.

"You're a nerd. And you believe in nerds. Your country is crowded with nerds. And my country too. I can't give you more than a sigh! Attention: SIGH!"

That wasn't very helpful, Honest Beggar. Thank you very much, indeed. Well, have a nice stay in room 40.

"Stop being so cruel to yourself. You want to be more free from the hatred of unethical pressure? You want to be near the home of us all, am I right, buddy? Those are your problems, aren't they? You just want to know whether love is the meaning of your life, don't you?"

Yes. But would you mind speaking more slowly, please?

"Do you know Raingirl?"

Yes. She is my great-grandmother.

"She is a witch. She is as old as this planet. Be careful, man."

Stop speaking. I'm not interested in listening to you any longer.

"I'll say it again. Don't be cruel to yourself. Now listen! You obviously have a problem with the rules of the world – with capitalistic economies and their supporters that lie within governments and parliaments around the world. You had missed the human power of changing this kind of world while being a leaf."

Oh. Yes. That's true.

"Sorry, but you will never be the savior of the whole planet. Never. Okay? So, try to calm down. Prefer the love."

Hmm. You are a weird one, sir.

"Ha! Now to the basics. The economy needs money and money needs endless winners who are able to create steady growth. These winners must be active, aggressive, greedy, pitiless and dominant. They are even ready to run risks. But they're just zombies. Okay?"

Go on. But – I am interested in love too, sir.

"In their world no life matters. All the other parts of human life, like saving the earth must be the primary job of human beings like you, buddy. That's much more important than your private yearning for love!"

Nevertheless, I think the economy could be important for all people worldwide. It has brought prosperity and progress to a lot of them.

"Listen. One day I spoke with Reagan and Thatcher. It was the day after they had done some deals with the economy, giving them authority. Since that time people changed into objects, only valued as workers and needed as consumers."

May I ask a question?

"No. Not yet. In reality, they never tried to come to an understanding before pulling away freedom and democratic rights. Change this, boy, roll it back. Try it if you feel strong enough."

Sigh.

"Living as a leaf is a very good idea, so soft and peaceful, but don't forget the planet needs people and an endless power to survive. Love is only a part of it."

Sigh.

"What did you say?"

Nothing. I only sighed. I won't be a leaf any longer. To be honest, I failed.

"Sorry, but to sigh isn't enough action. We all knew we could do what had seemed impossible. Why do you accept that the economy dominates your society and your life? Why do you accept the offer 'All you can eat'? So you allow the rulers of the economy to drive you and your children up the wall. For money. Basically, it's always for money, no matter what they tell you. They are washing away your humanity."

Rats!

"Stay cool, boy. The economy doesn't have any restrictions on humanity and peace. Look at their vocabulary! Look at these people and their faces! They will never be able to find the way out of their patriarchal Zoo without help. So don't stop trying, it's important for you and for the planet, too."

Rats!

"What did you say? Speak louder!"

I said rats!

"Ha! No rats, they took what they were given. Kick snowballs but be cautious of how dangerous they can be when they grow up and become avalanches!"

I'm getting a little tired. Thanks for your explanation, Honest Beggar. Now I'll put my body on the floor, so I can't fall down.

CHAPTER 11

"Wait a minute!" Then Honest Beggar turned to more personal matters.

"What a wonderful winter feeling outside. It's just snowing. It's great! I remember when I was a child. I always needed somebody to lean on."

You? Are you sure?

"I was always afraid of the future, ha."

And what do you think about it today?

"Figures I spoke about are on earth since the darkest past. If you had any light in your room, buddy, you could see one of them in a mirror, ha."

There was a long pause. Mr. Nor Lung knocked on the wall and asked in a loud voice,

Is there anything wrong, Mr. Beggar? Do you need help?

"The world and the economy have to go until the end." Mr. Beggar laughed and laughed.

What's wrong Mr. Beggar?

"No problems on my side of the wall. It's only the white snow covering the garden, buddy, all the trees and the fountain. My window is open, so some snowflakes are coming in."

Would you mind speaking louder, sir?

"Don't say 'sir' to me. There is no reason to die for fear of life. Look at me! If I were to know that a big terrible bomb will be ending the world tomorrow, I would father a child this very night and take it with me in the hope of peace afterwards."

Oh –

"Hahahahaha!"

Oh –

"Don't say 'oh' again, for it is well known that in our world the winner takes it all, even the truth."

Are you a winner, Honest Beggar?

"Not yet, otherwise I wouldn't stay in this damned residence."

Oh – um – sorry for saying 'oh'.

"Listen! Never give up, boy! You must fight! But attention! You never will win a fight against some of these powerful rich people. There's no chance for you, they are too many and too big. But you can fight for your life as a human of both genders and for the lives of all you love."

I'm on my way to try it, Mr. Beggar. Thanks for your sympathy. You really are an honourable man. I apologize for calling you Cissie Trump last year and for teasing you as a didgeridoo man. Sorry, sir.

"Didgeridoo? Ha. You are welcome. – Oh, what's this? There is a bird sitting on my windowsill. It's so funny. I never saw a bird nearby."

Mr. Nor Lung was surprised when Mr. Beggar spoke with a childish voice,

"Oh. I must be quiet now, for in my room there is so much snow. Snow and a bird, buddy. I really can't stand it!"

Mr. Nor Lung was more and more irritated. He wanted to speak with this man in number 40. So he asked,

Mr. Beggar, are these my choices: escape and hide as a leaf or stand up for myself?

"Hello, buddy, I have just seen a bird calling me!"

Mr. Beggar, are these my choices? Tell me!

"Hi, buddy, what a fascinating bird!"

Mr. Nor Lung was very irritated now. What was so interesting about some snow and a stupid bird?

A few minutes later the voice came again from behind the wall, obviously not intended for Mr. Nor Lung,

"The bird! Where is the bird? Is it gone? I am missing you, birdie. Why don't you trust a loser? Where are you?"

Mr. Beggar, do you have a problem? May I come and help you?

There came no answer.

Some minutes later Mr. Nor Lung heard a gentle voice singing. He was surprised to realize it was the voice of the former didgeridoo man,

"Little bird / I love you little bird / I love your eyes / I love your singing / with the sun / in the rain / your sleeping / with the moon / your flying among the fallen snow / under a great and cloudy / sky."

Mr. Nor Lung, still sitting on the floor, shut his eyes and felt himself relax, no longer noticing the darkness. He let his tears come and go. What is it about this Honest Beggar?

Number 40 repeated the song again and again until he finally allowed a great stillness to spread out. From now on there was only absolute silence in room 40.

Before he fell asleep Mr. Nor Lung promised himself,

What a wonderful world. If it shall be my destiny to stay on earth as a female human leaf I will do so for the rest of my life. But if my destiny is instead to fight for myself and the planet as a man with female feelings, I will do so too.

End of Part Two

Part Three

Reconsiliation

CHAPTER 12

Mr. Nor Lung was abruptly awoken by the three candles on the Christmas tree. They were lit up, sparkling in the dark room.

Raingirl? Are you in my room? Please, give me a sign.

A light laugh came from behind the tree. He first saw Raingirl's long blonde hair. Her entire being was transparent, almost like a ghost. Mr. Nor Lung looked at her face, full of respect and tenderness.

"Why are you crying, my love?" Raingirl asked in surprise.

I lost my burden this night and I am so glad to see you again.

Because there was no physical hand to take, Mr. Nor Lung could touch only something like fog between the tree branches. His young great-grandmother came closer and closer to him. He wanted to hold her in his arms but her body was not solid, leaving him with a weird feeling. It was impossible for him to touch her.

When Raingirl realized his troubles, she explained,

"You can't give me a hug, my dear, I'm out of time, you know. There is no way to change it and no chance of stopping it. Don't be so sorrowful. Life has to pass by like wonderful moments."

Tears formed in her eyes, but Mr. Nor Lung wasn't able to see them.

Then she laughed and bit him on his ear, sturdy and powerful. Mr. Nor Lung felt nothing. Unawares to him, women from more than twenty thousand years ago used this gesture as the most tender proof of their love. In this moment, Raingirl felt so happy as if she were his favorite sister.

Mr. Nor Lung continued to feel befuddled as the first candle went out.

CHAPTER 13

"Always trust in life, my love. It's still a wonderful world with sun and rain, fog and storms, sleep and animation, with lots of fun and so much never ending love."

I don't know whether this can be true. Sometimes I feel so terribly lonely, like I could just be washed away.

"The world is your only home. There is no other home for you as a male, female or human leaf. It's not necessary to lay on the ground in this room all day long."

I never asked you, my Raingirl, about your former life as my great-grandmother. Honest Beggar said you were a witch. I am filled by so much sorrow that you will leave me again without a last embrace.

"Life is only a constant change in limited settings, you know, like waking up after anesthesia. In fact, the world is a trap, an illusory one, so don't look behind."

If you are a witch, can you see the end of my life?

"Forget the 'witch'. Honest Beggar is a kind of eye opener, my son, but not always a truth seeker."

So, you can't see the end of my life?

"Why would I be able to? Your life is in God's hand and even mainly in your own."

When Raingirl said this the second candle went out.

CHAPTER 14

When the second candle went out a little hole appeared in the wall, revealing a small piece of the blue sky outside.

Suddenly a grey bird slipped in through the hole and into room 39. It flew around, slapping against the walls. When it bounced against the door, Mr. Nor Lung heard something that sounded suspiciously like "damn".

The bird eventually sat down in the small window aperture, shaking its feathers.

The young Raingirl giggled and quipped,

"Maybe it's Mr. Beggar from number 40. It seems to be his kind of hectic flight."

Honest Beggar as a bird? Where did you learn to speak so sarcastically?

"What's your problem, dear son? All is possible. All can become reality. Everywhere there are doors – or windows – to enter from and holes to leave by."

Mr. Nor Lung stared at her.

"Your existence is a gift of love, of my own love too", she continued. "Never forget this when you're feeling low. We all need compassion in the end."

With these parting words, she began to dissolve, until she had disappeared altogether.

Mr. Nor Lung cried a long cry.

CHAPTER 15

As Raingirl vanished, two birds sat in the window aperture. One was a plain grey and the other looked like a titmouse.

The grey bird shook its feathers before pushing off from the hole into the blue sky making the third candle flicker.

Now only the titmouse remained. It sat motionless but looked on with a friendly look in its eyes. Mr. Nor Lung thought,

Is this little bird watching me? It doesn't seem anxious...

He came closer to the hole, step by step. The bird continued looking at him.

Mr. Nor Lung had suddenly begun to notice an unknown power in his body when the last candle went out. He became extraordinarily calm and felt ready to change his body at will.

Belatedly, he recognized himself sitting on the windowsill next to the titmouse, looking back into his murky room number 39.

His nose was now so close to the titmouse that he could smell its slight scent, making him feel relaxed.

He had changed into a handsome black crow. There was no doubt in his mind, however, that he was still himself but in another body.

The little bird pushed its beak between the feathers of the crow,

Mr. Nor Lung watched the little bird and followed when it took flight.

They left the residence behind – it was no longer important. The sky outside was still blue, the air fresh and full of spring. The titmouse was waiting at the top of the fountain.

The crow's very last memory as Mr. Nor Lung was that of worry.

Don't leave me –

Even as he repeated this thought his mind had already started to become happy and full of possibilities for the future. He simply let his sorrow go. Thereby the crow lost the meaning of this sentence.

It even didn't remember that these words are human words.

End of Part Three

Part Four

Back Home

CHAPTER 16

They made their way south through woods, mountains, full countries and even a rough sea with little boats driving north. Though small, the boats were crowded with people.

The crow didn't have any emotions when looking down, for it didn't understand what exactly was going on there. But the titmouse, who did understand, informed it,

"Your forefathers did it likewise, long ago."

Why?

"Oh, they were hungry, that's all. Without their journey north they wouldn't have had a chance to survive. Perhaps your people will also do this southward journey sometime."

Okay, but now I need all my power in order to move my wings for I have to carry you on my back.

"We both can't help them, dear, for we are birds. I saw so much sorrow in my life and much more over the thousands of years after my life had ended. It was never possible for me to help. But you could do it, son, you are still alive. In fact, perhaps you must do it!"

As a leaf? Or as a bird?

"Be careful. The water below is deep and full of death."

The sea seemed endless. They flew and flew. After a while the crow asked the titmouse,

I never asked you how old you are, Raingirl. Besides, I wonder whether you understand the meaning of our modern lifestyle.

The water below was glittering in the sun. Finally the titmouse said,

"My birth was very long ago, more than twenty thousand years in the past. My mother said my first tears had been shed during a rainstorm. Therefore, as you know, she called me 'Raingirl'."

The black crow slowly moved its powerful wings slowly. It seemed impossible that the titmouse had really come from such a far past. The crow asked,

Where exactly were you coming from to help me? It can't be this planet! Did you come out of the universe?

The titmouse flew upwards before crawling once again onto the back of the crow. It let out a long sigh und whispered,

"Not really. I'm simply present, that's all."

And my world? Isn't it great?

"Try to trust your forefathers. They will be with you for as long as new life is born from your own and theirs within your shared lineage. You understand what I mean?"

I would like to hear what you think about my world. Is it not strange for a woman out of the past?

"It does not seem strange to me, my love. The people of your era are like the people I had known when I was still alive."

But all our skyscrapers, planes, cars, televisions?

"That's all not really important. People are the same. They have only different backgrounds and clothes and other ways of living. Only one thing is new and great: your music. The wonderful feeling when hundreds of people are singing all together."

The crow moved its powerful wings slowly up and down. It said,

Oh. What about freedom, prosperity, democracy?

"Words."

Words?

"Words from the ground of an ocean made of air."

A convulsion suddenly overtook the crow as the titmouse left his back, making it drop from his high flight. The titmouse had to carry the crow back into the sky.

CHAPTER 17

At long last the sea was coming to an end, they began to fly over a wide sandy land.

It became night. There were no lights down on the desert but a lot of stars above them. The crow became insecure.

I haven't seen any leaves since reaching this desert. Why are we flying over this poor landscape?

"Forget the leaf, son. Long ago, when I lived here as a young girl, there was no desert around. It was a green land with enough water and food for us all."

A soft wind blew onto the two birds.

Suddenly the titmouse flew very close to the body of the black crow and said,

"It was here that I was born. My baby too."

The crow tried to answer, but the only noise which came out of its beak was,

Caw! Caw!

The titmouse flew in a slow circle. Then another and another one. The crow continued to follow the little bird.

The titmouse said to the crow,

"Don't move your wings any longer, son. It was a long and exhausting flight. Now the wind will bring you back home."

The crow answered, *Caw!* – louder and louder – *Caw! Caw! Caw!*

But the titmouse had already slipped away. There was only a grey shadow left high above between the stars.

CHAPTER 18

It was a long flight back home, over several days and nights.

One morning the black crow reached a garden, a house and a fountain. Feeling very tired from its journey, it made to sit down at the top of the fountain. This was a mistake.

The crow knocked its head vehement against the fountain and promptly lost all its feathers. He wound up sitting in the water basin with water sprinkling down onto his tender, aching head.

A group of children came running to see what had happened, laughing all the while.

The bicycle driver stopped by once more, calling,

"Hi, weird fellow, did you have another foolish vision today?"

Mr. Nor Lung was very angry.

He left the basin and then touched his face. He was surprised to find a nose instead of a beak.

He laid down in a flowery meadow nearby and fell asleep at once.

CHAPTER 19

Mr. Nor Lung opened his eyes. In front of him stood a young woman. She had long blonde hair.

With a slight smile she asked,

"Excuse me, sir, sorry for waking you up. Would you please be so kind as to tell me whether you know anything about that house behind you?"

Mr. Nor Lung stood up.

Anything? About this house? Are you sure?

"Oh, yes, I am. In fact, I am glad you've woken up in time, sir. Now we can visit this house together."

End

Also by klaus landahl

(In German language)

'*Der Ruf des Lebens hört niemals auf*' (2018)
Second edition (2020)
The Neverending Cry of Life / Stories
ISBN 978-3-7407-6390-9

'*Rattenwette*' (2019)
Rat Bet / Fiction
ISBN 978-3-7407-5246-0

'*Unsere Demokratie auf Geisterfahrt*' (2019)
What's Wrong with our Democracy?
Nonfiction
ISBN 978-3-7407-6244-5

All printed by
Random House / Twentysix, Germany